THREE UP A TREE

THREE UP A TREE

by James Marshall

PUFFIN BOOKS

PUFFIN BOOKS
Published by the Penguin Group
Penguin Books USA Inc., 375 Hudson Street, New York, New York 10014, U.S.A.
Penguin Books Ltd, 27 Wrights Lane, London W8 5TZ, England
Penguin Books Australia Ltd, Ringwood, Victoria, Australia
Penguin Books Canada Ltd, 10 Alcorn Avenue, Toronto, Ontario, Canada M4V 3B2
Penguin Books (N.Z.) Ltd, 182-190 Wairau Road, Auckland 10, New Zealand

Penguin Books Ltd, Registered Offices: Harmondsworth, Middlesex, England

First published in the United States of America by Dial Books for Young Readers,
a division of Penguin Books USA Inc., 1986
First trade paperback edition published by Dial Books for Young Readers, 1989
Published in a Puffin Easy-to-Read edition, 1994

10

THE LIBRARY OF CONGRESS HAS CATALOGED THE DIAL EDITION AS FOLLOWS:

Marshall, James, 1942-1992
Three up a tree.
Summary: Sam and Spider build a tree house and go there with Lolly to trade stories.
[1. Storytelling—Fiction. 2. Tree Houses—Fiction.] I. Title.
ISBN 0-8037-0328-7(tr.) ISBN 0-8037-0329-5(lib. bdg.) ISBN 0-14-036216-9(pb.)
PZ7.M35672Th 1986 [E] 86-2163

Puffin Easy-to-Read ISBN 0-14-037003-X

Printed in the United States of America

Reading Level 1.8

For Toby Sherry

KEEP OUT
!!!

"Wow!" said Spider.

"Will you look at *that*!"

Some big kids down the street

had built a swell tree house.

"Can we come up?" called out Sam.

"No!" said the big kids.

"Well!" said Spider.

"Never mind," said Sam.

"We'll build our own tree house."

"Let's ask Lolly to help,"

said Spider.

But Lolly would not help.

"I'm too busy," she said.

"You call *that* busy?" said Spider.

"Let's go," said Sam.

In no time Spider and Sam
were as busy as squirrels.
Meanwhile Lolly decided
to take a little snooze.

When Lolly woke up
the tree house was finished.
"Wow," she said.
"I'll be right up."
"Oh, no," said Sam.
"You didn't help."
"Oh, *please*," said Lolly.
"No!" said Spider.
"I know some good stories,"
said Lolly.
"Stories?" said Sam.
"I love a good story."

KEEP OUT
KEEP OUT

Lolly was up the tree in a flash.

"Now tell us a story," said Sam.

"And make it good," said Spider.

"Sit down," said Lolly.

"And listen to this."

Lolly's Story

One summer evening
a doll and a chicken
went for a walk.
And they got lost.
"Oh, no," said the doll.

Just then a monster
came around the corner.
"Oh, no," said the doll.
"Let's run!"
cried the chicken.

And they ran as fast
as they could.
"He's right behind us!"
cried the chicken.
"Oh, no!"
said the doll.

"Quick!" cried the chicken.

"Let's climb that tree!"

And they did—

in a jiffy.

But monsters know how

to climb trees too.

“He’s got us now!” cried the chicken.

“Oh, no!” cried the doll.

The monster opened his mouth.

"Will you tie my new shoes?"

he said.

"Oh, yes!" said the doll.

"Not much of a story,"

said Spider.

"The end was too sweet."

"Can you tell a better story?"

said Lolly.

"Listen to this," said Spider.

Spider's Story

A chicken caught the wrong bus.
She found herself
in a bad part of town—
the part of town where foxes live.
"Uh-oh," she said.

Quickly she pulled down her hat
and waited for the next bus.
But very soon—you guessed it—
a hungry fox came along
and sat beside her.

His eyes were not good.

But there was nothing wrong

with his nose.

"I can smell that you're having

chicken tonight," he said.

"Er. . ." said the chicken.

"Yes, I have just been to the store."

"I *love* chicken,"

said the fox.

"How will you cook it?"

The chicken knew
she had to be clever.
She did not want the fox
to invite himself to dinner.
"Well," she said.
"I always cook my chicken
in sour chocolate milk
with lots of pickles and rotten eggs."
"It sounds delicious,"
said the fox.
"May I come to dinner?"

“Let’s see,” said the chicken.
“That will make ten of us.”
Well, *that* was too many
for the fox!
He grabbed the chicken’s grocery bag
and ran away.
“All for me!” he cried.
“All for me!”

The poor chicken flew up
into a nearby tree
to wait for the next bus.
(She should have done that
in the first place.)

P.S. When the fox got home,

he reached into the bag.

But there was no chicken inside.

Only the chicken's favorite food.

Can you guess what it was?

"Worms!" cried Lolly. "Worms!
That story wasn't bad."
"Not bad at all," said Sam.
"But now it's *my* turn."

Sam's Story

A monster woke up from a nap.

He was *very* hungry.

"I want ice cream," he said.

"Lots of it."

He went out to buy some.

But he got lost.

“Oh, well,” he said.

“I’ll just ask someone for help.”

At that moment a fox

came around the corner.

"Excuse me," said the monster.

"Help!" cried the fox.

"I'm getting out of here!"

And away he went.

"How rude," said the monster.

He put on the fox's hat,

scarf, and glasses.

Just then a doll and a chicken

came around the corner.

"Hi," said the chicken.

“Will you help me find
some ice cream?” said the monster.
“If you will give us a ride
in your wagon,” said the chicken.
And off they went.

“Stop!” said the chicken.

“This is the place for ice cream.”

“Oh really?” said the monster.

“Wait here,” said the doll.

“We’ll be right back.”

In a moment they were back.

"Step on it!" said the doll.

"You don't want your ice cream
to melt!"

"I'll hurry!" said the monster.

"Faster!" cried the chicken.

The monster ran as fast as he could.

Soon they came to a big tree.

"This is where we live,"

said the doll.

And they all climbed up the tree.
The doll and the chicken
opened their bags.
But there was
no ice cream inside.
There was only money.
"Oh, no!" said the monster.
"You are bank robbers!"

The monster took off his hat,
scarf, and glasses.
The doll and the chicken
were scared out of their wits.

"Help, help!" they cried.
"Let's get out of here!"
And they ran as fast as their
little legs could carry them.

The monster returned
the money to the bank.
As a reward he was given
all the ice cream he could eat.
And there was *lots* of it!

"My story was better," said Lolly.

"No, mine was," said Spider.

"No, mine!" said Sam.

"Let's hear them again," said Lolly.

And they did.